Here Comes the TOOTH FAIRY CAT

Here Comes
the
TOOTH FAIRY

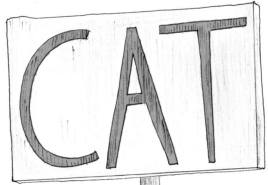

CAT

by
DEBORAH UNDERWOOD

pictures by
CLAUDIA RUEDA

Dial Books for Young Readers
an imprint of Penguin Group (USA) LLC

Cat! You lost a tooth!

Did the Tooth Fairy come?

She left you a coin!

What's the matter?

You wanted to meet her?

Aw, Cat. I understand.
Too bad she only comes when
you've lost a tooth, huh?

Oh, boy.
What are you up to?

You're going to leave her the tooth of a *comb*?

Cat, I don't think you should try to trick a fairy.

Cat? Did you hear me?

Oh, dear.

Good night, Cat. I hope you're
not making a mistake.

Good morning, Cat!

The Tooth Fairy didn't come?
Well, I'm not too surprised.

Hey—who's at the door?

DING
DONG

Look at that!

What does the card say?

Dear Cat,
Nice try with the comb. I am the Tooth Fairy, not the Tooth Hairy. But if you help me with a few deliveries, maybe we can meet.

Love, Tooth Fairy

How about that! You'll be the
Tooth Fairy Cat!

Better try on your costume.

Um . . . wow.

Hey, what's that note?

P.S. You'll have some help.

TOOTH FAIRY COSTUME

Huh. I wonder what that means.

Oh, my.

Uh . . . hello, Mouse.

Did you try to trick the
Tooth Fairy too?

Looks like you two have
a lot in common!

So who's first on the Tooth Fairy's list?

Hmm. I wonder if a certain
fairy is watching.

Looks like you have three
stops to make—you'd better
get going!

What is it, Cat?

No, you may *not* eat the mouse.

Your first stop is a gopher?

Cat, you'd have a hard time getting down that hole.

Good thing Mouse is here.

Cat! Mouse can climb into the hole perfectly well without your, uh, help.

You got the tooth!
Nice work, Mouse!

Who's next?

A squirrel? Wow, that nest is pretty high. This looks like a job for Cat.

Cats are very good climbers, Mouse. We won't need a cannon.

Great work, Cat!

Who's going to get the last tooth?

Wait . . . whose tooth is it?

It's a *bear's* tooth?!

I don't think either of you should do this. It sounds too dangerous!

Mouse! That's very
brave of you.

Wow, Cat. Mouse has been in there a long time, huh?

I hope everything's okay!

Oh no! Mouse's skirt is stuck under the bear!

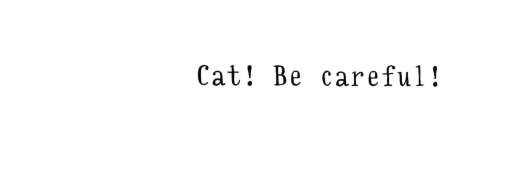

Cat! Be careful!

HOORAY!

Sorry! I mean, hooray!

Tickling the bear was a
brilliant idea, Cat!

Great work, you two!

Now I guess it's time to pack up
your Tooth Fairy costumes.

Mouse? Aren't you going to take
off your costume?

Oh, my goodness!

See, Cat? Fairies are very tricky!

That's why it's so hard to trick *them*!

Wow, Cat! You get to keep the bear's tooth!

Hey, let me take a photo for your scrapbook.

Bye, Tooth Fairy!

I'll bet Cat won't be tricking
you again any time soon!

You want to see the picture?

Of course! Let's take a look.

Oh, Cat.

For Bella. Of course. —D.U.

For the Raton Perez, just in case. —C.R.

Dial Books for Young Readers
Published by the Penguin Group • Penguin Group (USA) LLC • 375 Hudson Street, New York, New York 10014

USA / Canada / UK / Ireland / Australia / New Zealand / India / South Africa / China
PENGUIN.COM
A Penguin Random House Company

Text copyright © 2015 by Deborah Underwood • Pictures copyright © 2015 by Claudia Rueda

Library of Congress Cataloging-in-Publication Data
Underwood, Deborah.   Here comes the Tooth Fairy Cat / by Deborah Underwood ; pictures by Claudia Rueda.   pages cm
Summary: "Cat tries to trick the Tooth Fairy, but he meets his match in a mischievous mouse" — Provided by publisher.
ISBN 978-0-525-42774-2 (hardcover)   [1. Cats—Fiction. 2. Mice—Fiction. 3. Tooth fairy—Fiction. 4. Humorous stories.]
I. Rueda, Claudia, illustrator. II. Title.
PZ7.U4193Hft 2015   [E]—dc23   2014025759

Manufactured in China on acid-free paper

10 9 8 7 6 5 4 3 2 1

Designed by Jennifer Kelly • Text set in Handwriter OT

The publisher does not have any control over
and does not assume any responsibility for
author or third-party websites or their content.

THE ART WAS MADE WITH INK AND COLOR
PENCILS ON WHITE PAPER, SURROUNDED
BY HUNDREDS OF CATS (INK CATS!).